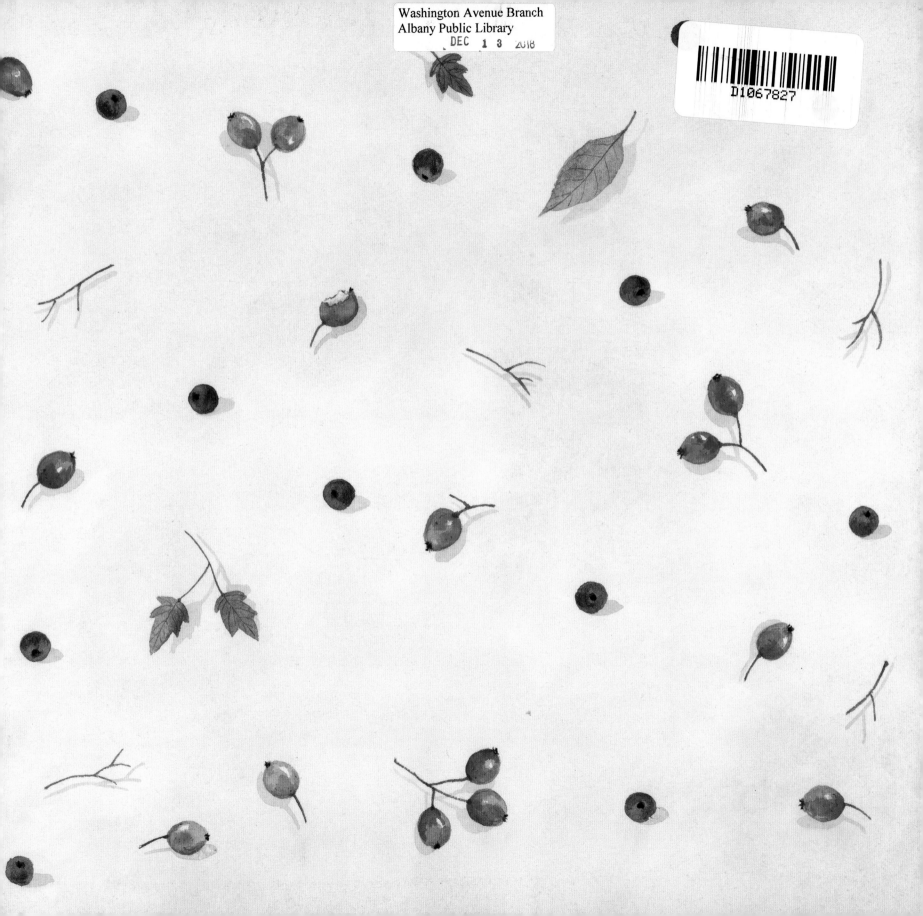

minedition

English edition published 2017 by Michael Neugebauer Publishing Ltd., Hong Kong

Michael Neugebauer Publishing Ltd.,
Unit 28, 5/F, Metro Centre, Phase 2, No.21 Lam Hing Street,
Kowloon Bay, Kowloon, Hong Kong.
Phone +852 2807 1711, e-mail: info@minedition.com
This edition was printed in July 2018 at L.Rex Printing Co Ltd.
3/F., Blue Box Factory Building, 25 Hing Wo Street,
Tin Wan, Aberdeen, Hong Kong, China
Typesetting in Papyrus
Library of Congress Cataloging-in-Publication Data available upon request.

ISBN 978-988-8341-52-8
10 9 8 7 6 5 4 3 2

For more information please visit our website: www.minedition.com

Kate Westerlund **A Whisper in the Snow**

with pictures by Feridun Oral

minedition

"I am not making it up," said Kip. "This is where I heard the whisper come out of the snow."

"Snow doesn't whisper," said Wally.

"What did it say?" asked Agnes.

"It said it was lost. Shh, I think I hear it again."

"I don't hear anything," said Wally.

"Let's dig," said Bella and Bob together. The mice often said the same thing at the same time. They were twins.

"That's the strangest looking bear I've ever seen," said Wally.

"It's a teddy," said Kip.

"Just look at him," said Bella and Bob. "He's all freezy-frozen."

"Where do you belong, little bear?" asked Agnes.

"He can't talk," said Wally. "His mouth is only stitched on. How could you hear him whisper, Kip?"

"Well, I hear it when my teddy whispers."

"We can't just leave him here," said Agnes.

"Where can we take him?" asked Wally.

"I have an idea," said Agnes.

They loaded the teddy in the wagon. Wally and Agnes pulled, and Kip pushed.
Bella and Bob held the teddy's paw so he wouldn't be frightened.
"Where are we going?" asked Wally.
"We're going to Arthur's," said Agnes.
"Arthur's! But he's so grumpy when you wake him in winter," said Wally.
"That's why I'm going to get some honey; Arthur loves it," said Agnes.

Agnes walked directly to the front door with a basket and knocked.

"Who's there?" roared a voice.

"Arthur, it's Agnes. We've brought you some Christmas honey."

The door opened slowly, squeaking on its hinges.

"And we have a 'We-don't-know-what- to-do' question," said Kip.

"Then you better come in," said Arthur, taking the jar of honey and marching back into his house.

"What is that poor thing?" asked Arthur.

"That's our question," said Agnes. "We found it—I mean him—buried in the snow."

"Kip heard a whisper or something," said Wally.

"Not something—I heard a whisper, and it said it was lost," said Kip. "But now he won't talk. What should we do?"

"Oh my," said the big bear, taking a closer look. "And on the day before Christmas, a child is without his or her beloved bear."

"How do you know he was loved?" asked Agnes.

"Just look at him," said Arthur with a sigh. "He's been dragged everywhere; one button eye is missing, and he's been squeezed and loved so hard that his fur has rubbed off in places, and some of his stuffing has come out."

"Maybe a dog got after it," said Bella and Bob, "or a cat!"

"No, I think this bear has just been a companion for a long time," said Arthur.

"Maybe the child will get a new bear for Christmas?" said Wally.

"It's possible, but it won't be the same," said Arthur.

"He looks terrible," said Agnes, "and now that he's thawing out, he's all soggy."

"Put him in the rocking chair by the fire so he can dry out," said Arthur.

"Couldn't we do something, at least to make him look better for Christmas?" asked Kip.

"That's a wonderful idea," said Arthur, "let's see what you can find at home to help this poor bear. But hurry back, there's a lot to do. And Agnes, is there a bit more of that delicious Christmas honey?"

"My old vest looks great," said Wally. "And I brought a ribbon we can use as a tie."

"Mom gave me these little squares to use for patches, so he doesn't lose any more stuffing," said Agnes.

"We have a button for his missing eye. We can sew it on if someone will help us," said Bob.

"And what did you find, Kip?" said Arthur.

"A jingle bell," answered Kip.

"But that's your favorite bell," said Agnes.

"I think he needs it more than I do," said Kip.

"What's the safety pin for?" asked Arthur.

"I was going to pin the bell to the vest, in case he gets lost again," said Wally.

"Marvelous!" roared Arthur. "I'll ask the crow to gather all his bird friends and fly along the edge of the woods, where the people live. Maybe they can find an unhappy child who might be missing a teddy bear."

"Look, I think the bear is smiling," said Kip.

"He looks great," said Wally. "Not exactly new, but…"

"Better than new," said Kip. "Hey, what's that noise?"

"The birds," said Agnes.

"Are they back already?" Arthur wondered. "I hope they have good news. Did anyone find the child who might be missing this bear?"

"I did, I think," said the crow. "In a house on the other side of the river, there's a little girl who just sits at the window and cries."

"How do we get the bear to the girl?" asked Kip.

"It's Christmas Eve," said Wally. "We could put him down the chimney."

"Then he would be just as messy as when we found him," said Agnes.

"The owl can fly the bear to the front door," said the crow, "and you can all watch from a distance.

"This is so exciting!" said Bella and Bob.

"Look, it really is her bear," said Arthur.

"They look so happy," said Agnes.

"I feel all Christmas-y," said Wally.

"Shh, I think I hear something," said Kip. "A whisper!"

"Is it the bear?" asked the twins. "What's he saying?"

"He says thank you all," said Kip, "and Merry Christmas!"